CW00400730

THE OLD MAN
and the
EDIBLE SUIT

("The New Vestments")

EDWARD LEAR

Illustrated by Jon Atlas Higham

M

MACMILLAN CHILDREN'S BOOKS

"The New Vestments" was first published in 1871 in *Nonsense Songs*

This edition first published 1986 by
MACMILLAN CHILDREN'S BOOKS
A division of Macmillan Publishers Limited London and Basingstoke Associated companies throughout the world

British Library Cataloguing in Publication Data
Lear, Edward
    [The new vestments]. The old man and the edible suit.
    I. [The new vestments] II. Title
    III. Higham, Jon Atlas
    821'.8   PR4879.L2

ISBN 0·333·41384·9

Printed in Hong Kong

There lived an old man in the Kingdom of Tess,
Who invented a purely original dress;

And when it was perfectly made and complete,
He opened the door, and walked into the street.

By way of a hat he'd a loaf of Brown Bread,

In the middle of which he inserted his head;—

His Shirt was made up of no end of dead Mice,

The warmth of whose skins was quite fluffy and nice;—

His Drawers were of Rabbit-skins;—so were his Shoes;—
His Stockings were skins,—but it is not known whose;—

His Waistcoat and Trowsers were made of Pork Chops;—
His Buttons were Jujubes, and Chocolate Drops;—

His Coat was all Pancakes with Jam for a border,

And a girdle of Biscuits to keep it in order;

And he wore over all, as a screen from bad weather,
A Cloak of green Cabbage-leaves stitched all together.

He had walked a short way, when he heard a great noise,
Of all sorts of Beasticles, Birdlings, and Boys;—

And from every long street and dark lane in the town
Beasts, Birdles, and Boys in a tumult rushed down.

Two Cows and a Calf ate his Cabbage-leaf Cloak;—

Four Apes seized his Girdle, which vanished like smoke;—

Three Kids ate up half of his Pancaky Coat,—

And the tails were devoured by an ancient He Goat;—

An army of Dogs in a twinkling tore *up* his

Pork Waistcoat and Trowsers to give to their Puppies;—

And while they were growling, and mumbling the Chops,

Ten Boys prigged the Jujubes and Chocolate Drops.—

He tried to run back to his house, but in vain,
For scores of fat Pigs came again and again;—

They rushed out of stables and hovels and doors,—
They tore off his stockings, his shoes, and his drawers;—

And now from the housetops with screechings descend,

Striped, spotted, white, black, and gray cats without end,

They jumped on his shoulders and knocked off his hat,—

When Crows, Ducks and Hens made a mince-meat of that;—

They speedily flew at his sleeves in a trice,

And utterly tore up his Shirt of dead Mice;—

They swallowed the last of his Shirt with a squall,—

Whereon he ran home with no clothes on at all.

And he said to himself as he bolted the door,
"I will not wear a similar dress any more,
"Any more, any more, any more, never more!"